Curious George®

GOES TO AN AIR SHOW

Adapted from the Curious George film series

Edited by Margret Rey and Alan J. Shalleck

SCHOLASTIC INC.

NEW YORK   TORONTO   LONDON   AUCKLAND   SYDNEY

ISBN 0-590-45295-9

Copyright © 1990 by Houghton Mifflin Company and Curgeo Agencies, Inc.
All rights reserved. Published by Scholastic Inc.,
730 Broadway, New York, NY 10003,
by arrangement with Houghton Mifflin Company.

12 11 10 9 8 7 6 5 4 3 2   2 3 4 5 6/9

Printed in the U.S.A.   24

First Scholastic printing, December 1991

"George," said his friend,
"there's an air show today at the airfield.
Let's go and watch."

They got into their little blue car
and drove to the airfield.

There were people and airplanes everywhere.

They ran into the manager, who looked worried.
"The sky divers haven't arrived yet,"
he said, "but the show must go on."

The man with the yellow hat stayed to talk
with the manager. "You can look around,"
he told George, "but stay out of trouble."

George watched the pilots and mechanics
getting their planes ready for the show.

Then George noticed a strange thing
hanging on a pole.

What was that? George was curious.

George climbed up the pole,
untied the funny thing,
and put it on his head.

"Hey! What's that monkey doing?"
yelled a pilot. "He took our wind sock."
"After him!" yelled a mechanic.

The pilot and mechanic ran after George.

George jumped into a plane to hide.

But then a pilot got into the plane that
George was in. He didn't see George.

He started the engine and took off.

Once the plane was high above the ground,
George peeked out.
"Where did you come from?" yelled the pilot.

George held onto the straps of a parachute
with his feet and leaned out to look.
Where was the man with the yellow hat?

Suddenly the plane did a loop . . .
and out went George!

"Oh my gosh!" shouted the pilot.
"What have I done?"

George was scared.

"Pull the string!" yelled the pilot.

George grabbed a string,
and the parachute popped open.

"Look!" someone on the ground shouted.
"A skydiving monkey!"
"Great show," someone else yelled.

George slowly floated down to earth.

At last he landed with the
parachute on top of him.

A mechanic and the manager
came running over.

"This is the monkey that took our wind sock,"
yelled the mechanic.

The manager came to George's rescue.
"Leave him alone," he said.
"George saved the show."

Everyone cheered and clapped.

The man with the yellow hat came over.
"I guess we got to see a sky diver after all."

"Here's something for you, George,"
said the manager.
"You've earned your wings."